Naya
The Inuit Cinderella

Written by
Brittany Marceau-Chenkie

Illustrations by
Shelley Brookes

Raven Rock Publishing
Yellowknife, NT

Dedication

To my mother, Michelle,
for passing on her love
of the North to me.
Brittany

Once upon a time, in the far North, there lived a girl named Naya. She lived on the land with her grandfather, Ataatatsiaq. Naya's mother, Aspak, and father, Akittiq, lived in the community of Igloolik. Naya's mother and father had two other daughters who names were Jochebed and Atagu. Unlike Naya, they did not care to learn the traditional ways of their elders so they stayed in Igloolik with their parents. Naya chose to live with her grandfather; she was very interested in carrying on the traditions of her ancestors. In winter time Naya could get from her grandfather's camp to Igloolik across the sea ice by dog team.

One night, while Naya was readying herself for bed, Ataatatsiaq told her: "The Igloolik Community Feast is coming up soon. Will you make a new dress or a traditional amauti to wear?"

"Oh, Grandfather, I live with you on the land in an igloo and live off what you can hunt. How can you even ask what I will wear!" replied Naya.

"Naya, I am glad you respect the old ways but you do not have a lot of time so you had better start work on your amauti as soon as possible. I will go in the morning to hunt the caribou so you will have hides to sew. Since your grandmother is no longer here you will have a lot of work to do to prepare the hides for sewing. They must be scraped and stretched before you can start your sewing and beadwork."

"Oh, yes, Grandfather. I will start as soon as you return from the hunt," Naya replied excitedly. She thought about the feast. Every year the community feast was celebrated and the young women of Igloolik wore their very best. For many of the young men and women who lived the traditional life on the land, this was their one chance to meet.

"Good. Now you must get to bed," insisted her grandfather.

That night, Naya tossed and turned. She was thinking about how lovely her hew amauti would look when it was finished. She knew that she could not go to the feast in anything less than the traditional parka worn by the Inuit women.

When she awoke the next day her grandfather had already left to hunt the caribou. When he returned that evening, Naya started her work right away, scraping and cleaning the hides. She had no time to waste, as the day of the feast was fast approaching, and she had so much to do. Cutting and sewing the hides did not take long, but the beadwork was all done by hand and required much time and patience to do. Naya's grandmother had been a skilled beadworker and had taught Naya all she could.

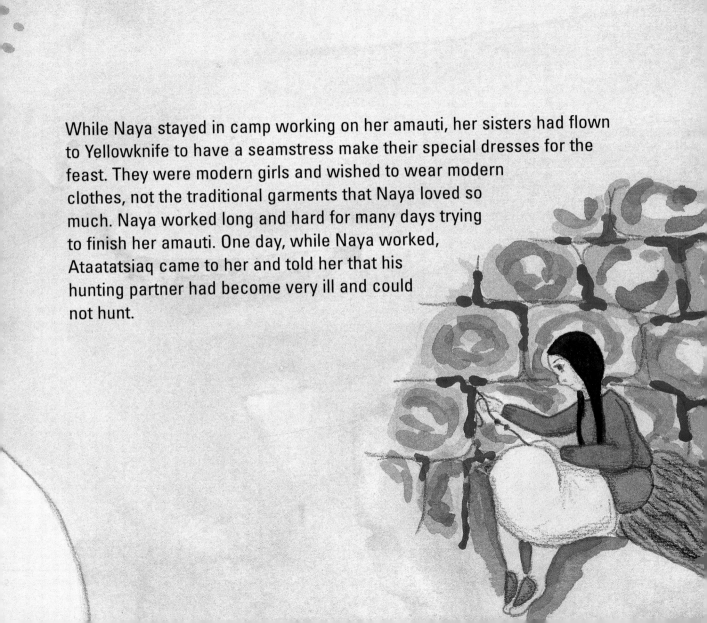

While Naya stayed in camp working on her amauti, her sisters had flown
to Yellowknife to have a seamstress make their special dresses for the
feast. They were modern girls and wished to wear modern
clothes, not the traditional garments that Naya loved so
much. Naya worked long and hard for many days trying
to finish her amauti. One day, while Naya worked,
Ataatatsiaq came to her and told her that his
hunting partner had become very ill and could
not hunt.

"Naya, I promised that we would bring caribou and seal meat for the feast but I cannot hunt without my partner," he lamented.

"Do not worry, Grandfather," answered Naya, "I'll come with you. Together we will hunt for the meat." Even as she said this Naya knew that if she went she would not have time to finish her amauti; but more importantly, Naya did not want her grandfather to go hunting alone.

Naya and Ataatatsiaq were many days on the hunt. They returned from the hunting trip on the day of the feast and Naya felt sad when she saw her unfinished amauti. She worked hard for the rest of the day while her grandfather delivered the meat to town, but she could not manage to finish the beadwork. Her amauti was not ready. Naya decided that she could not attend the feast in anything less than a beautifully made and finished amauti. She felt very sad; however, she decided to put on her unfinished amauti and wear it with great pride, even though she would go no further than outside the igloo.

When it was time for the feast to begin in Igloolik, she stepped outside her igloo and saw the northern lights dancing in the sky. It was the most beautiful show of lights that she had ever seen: a myriad of colours dancing in the dark of the evening. As she watched, the colours came closer and closer and began to swirl all around her body, then, just as quickly, they faded. When she looked down she saw that her amauti was completely finished, and that it had the most beautiful beadwork she had ever seen. Could it be her grandmother watching over her, wondered Naya, just as she had watched over her grandfather on the hunt? At the same time, a team of seven white sled dogs appeared, all harnessed in gold and pulling a golden komatik. Naya quickly jumped onto the magnificent komatik and away the dogs went.

The dogs knew exactly which way to go and after a magical ride they arrived at the feast. Naya was quick to enter the Community Hall, feeling so beautiful and proud.

Her sisters were there in their new dresses. They did not recognize Naya in her new amauti. They would never have believed that Naya would be able to sew anything so beautiful. Naya looked around the room seeing how happy everyone was and how many people swayed in time to the beating of the traditional drums. As she continued to look around the room, her eyes met with those of the most handsome hunter she had ever seen. In an instant, they were dancing together to the Inuit drums.

Before long, Naya realized that she must go; she had not told her grandfather that she was coming to the feast; he would be worried about her. Without even saying goodbye, she rushed out of the feast. As she pushed her way through the door, her amauti snagged on a sharp hook of caribou antler and a piece was torn from it. Naya did not have time to stop and worry about her amauti; she just kept running. Her magical dog sled whisked her off into the cold night. No sooner had she arrived home and stepped off the sled than suddenly her light-filled amauti shattered into a million pieces and the dog sled simply vanished.

The following day, the hunter was very disappointed. He had searched for Naya throughout the hall after she left and had asked many people for her name, but no one knew who the girl in the beautiful amauti had been. All he had was the small ripped piece of her amauti. He showed it to everyone but no one knew who it belonged to. Finally, one of the elders was shown the piece and recognized the stitching as that of Naya. The old woman told the hunter that Naya lived on the land with her grandfather, Ataatatsiaq, and where he might find her.

The hunter thanked the elder and set out right away to find Naya. It was not long before he came across the igloo where he was greeted by Ataatatsiaq. He was quick to ask Ataatatsiaq if he had a granddaughter named Naya. Just as Ataatatsiaq was about to answer, Naya appeared from behind him. Their eyes met once again and Naya had not forgotten the eyes of the handsome hunter from the feast.

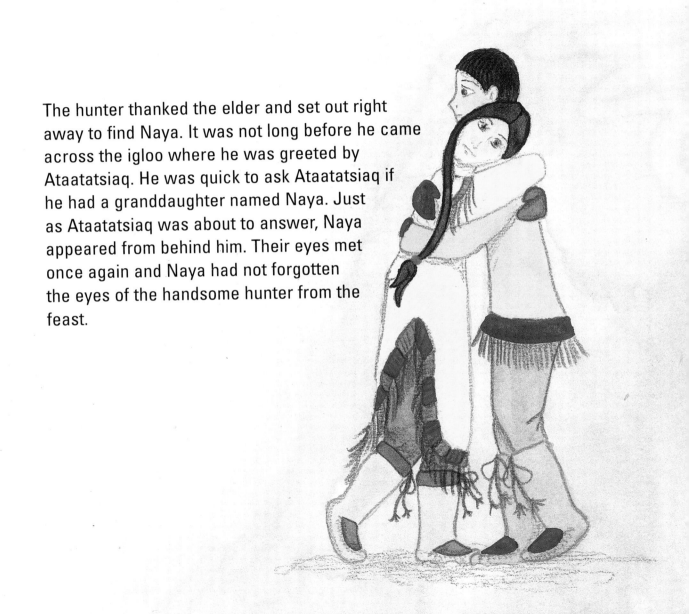

The hunter wasted no time in asking Ataatatsiaq for Naya's hand in marriage. Much to her delight, Ataatatsiaq consented. They were soon married and lived a traditional life on the land, happily ever after.